FRIENDS FUR LiFE

Hylas Publishing
129 Main Street
Irvington, New York 10533
www.hylaspublishing.com

Hylas Publishing
Editorial Director: Lori Baird
Art Directors: Edwin Kuo, Gus Yoo
Production Coordinator: Sarah Reilly

Project Credits
Editor: Sarah Reilly
Managing Editor: Myrsini Stephanides
Designer: Shani Parsons

ISBN: 1-59258-133-1

Library of Congress Cataloging-in-Publication Data
available upon request.

Printed and bound in Italy
Distributed by National Book Network

First American Edition published in 2005

10 9 8 7 6 5 4 3 2 1

FRIENDS FUR LIFE

HYLAS

WITH
A BEAR
BY YOUR SIDE,
THE ROAD
NEVER SEEMS
SO LONG

6

FURRY OR
FUZZY, A HUG
IS ALWAYS
BEARY NICE

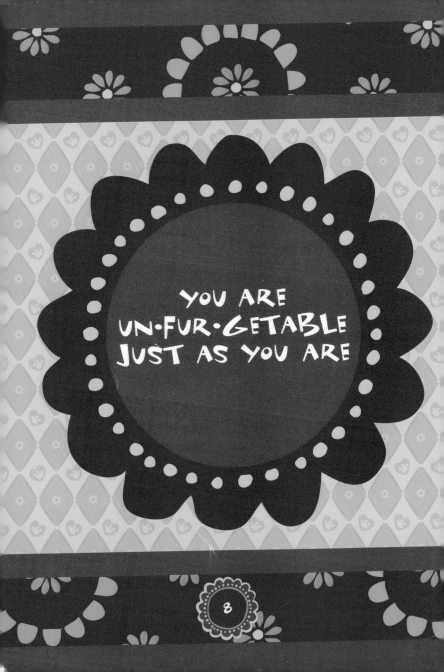

YOU ARE
UN·FUR·GETABLE
JUST AS YOU ARE

Best Friends are the Best Listeners

ONE GOOD BEAR DESERVES ANOTHER

14

A GOOD DAY
BECOMES
THE BEST DAY
WHEN SHARED
WITH A BEAR

Love is
The Beary Best
Gift That Keeps
on Giving

16

18

TRUE FRIENDS
SEE THE LOVE
INSIDE.
FRIENDS NEVER
LET YOU FUR·GET
WHO YOU
REALLY ARE

19

A BEAR WILL WALK A MILE FUR A FRIEND

SECRETS
ARE MEANT
TO BE SHARED
WITH YOUR
BEARY BEST
FRIEND

A BEAR
CAN ALWAYS
SHARE YOUR
DREAMS

A BEAR WILL GO TO THE DEPTHS FUR YOU

DON'T FUR·GET TO LEND A PAW TO A FRIEND IN NEED

HUGS ARE THE LANGUAGE OF FRIENDSHIP

OTHER BOOKS FROM HYLAS PUBLISHING IN THE BUILD·A·BEAR WORKSHOP® SERIES:

CELE·BEAR·ATE!

STUFFED WITH LOVE

PAWSITIVE THOUGHTS

BUILD·A·BEAR WORKSHOP®
FURRY FRIENDS HALL OF FAME
THE OFFICIAL COLLECTOR'S GUIDE

Hylas Publishing would like to thank Ginger Bandoni, Melissa Segal, Lori Zelkind, and Patty Sullivan at Evergreen Concepts. Many thanks to Laura Kurzu, Mindy Barsky, and of course, C.E.B. Maxine Clark.